D1175874

RAYSTOWN COUNTRY
RC
READING COUNCIL

The Listeners

Gloria Whelan

Illustrated by Mike Benny

SLEEPING BEAR PRESS

TALES *of* YOUNG AMERICANS SERIES

To Joseph and Michael McEvoy

—GLORIA

To my wonderful wife

—MIKE

The poem, "A Passionate Shepherd to His Love," is by Christopher Marlowe.

Sleeping Bear Press™
310 North Main Street, Suite 300
Chelsea, MI 48118
www.sleepingbearpress.com

Printed and bound in China.

First Edition

10 9 8 7 6 5 4 3 2 1

Library of Congress Cataloging-in-Publication Data

Whelan, Gloria.
The listeners / written by Gloria Whelan; illustrated by Mike Benny.
p. cm.
Summary: After a day of picking cotton in late 1860, Ella May, a young slave, joins her friends Bobby and Sue at their second job of listening outside the windows of their master's house for useful information.
ISBN 978-1-58536-419-0
[1. Slavery—Fiction. 2. African Americans—Fiction. 3. Listening—Fiction. 4. Southern States—History—1775-1865—Fiction.] I. Benny, Mike, 1964- ill. II. Title.
PZ7.W5718Lhw 2009
[E]—dc22
2009005436

Author's Note

The lives of slaves depended on circumstances beyond their control. They had nothing to say about whom they would work for or where they would live. They never knew when they might be separated from their children or their spouses. Hoping to learn their fate, they sent small children to hide near the windows of their masters' homes to listen.

Authors are listeners, too, that's how they find their stories. They listen. Sometimes they hear stories from people who have lived them. Sometimes they hear words spoken long ago and set down in books. It's what writers do; they listen, and like Bobby, Sue, and Ella May they pass the stories along.

It's still dark in the morning when the boss blows on the bugle. We're out of bed fast.

My friends, Bobby and Sue, are too little to pick cotton like I do. Bobby drives the cows out to pasture.

Sue helps the grannies care for the babies.

We come home tired. We come home hungry, but Bobby, Sue, and me, Ella May, got more work to do after supper.

We got to listen.

Sweet potatoes in our bellies, molasses still sweet on our mouths, we're on our way. Master and Mistress at the great house don't tell us slaves nothing. We children listen and carry back the news to our folk.

The fireflies turn on and off. Bobby, Sue, and me, Ella May, hunch down in the bushes next to the great house. Listening is a job for us children. We make ourselves small as cotton seeds and quiet as shadows.

The breezes puff the curtains out the open windows. Sand flies bite us and mosquitoes stick pins in us but we don't slap at them. We're here to listen.

Master Thomas and Mistress Louise and their children, little Master John and little Mistress Grace, are taking their leisure. Mistress Grace is playing on the piano. The music talks and talks to us and never has to say a word. We hold hands tight for fear the music's going to carry us right away.

Master Thomas tells the Mistress we slaves going to get us a new overseer to boss us. I got a smile big as an alligator's on my face. I hate the old boss. If you don't pick the cotton fast enough he comes by with his nasty cane and flicks it at you.

Bobby, Sue, and me, Ella May, hurry home fast as foxes to tell the news.

Our mammies clap hands and dance around. My daddy says, “I’m not clapping my hands ’til I see the new man.”

The sun and me start our work at the same time. I pick with Mammy and Daddy. The little prickers on the cotton plants bite at my fingers. We work hard in the cool of the morning. Daddy once picked four hundred pounds of cotton in one day. Nobody picks faster than my daddy does.

It’s noon and time to eat. There’s a big wooden trough for us kids and clamshells for spoons. We got salt pork and corn dumplings, and a mess of black-eyed peas lookin’ up at us. We eat and eat until our bellies are fat as possums.

In the afternoon the sun melts me so I can hardly pick. Daddy sees my basket is nearly empty and he puts in some of his cotton. He doesn’t want the boss to flick me with his nasty cane.

That night up at the great house we listen and hear Master Thomas say, "I've had an offer from the Spencers to buy William. They're short of men."

William! That's my daddy! My heart's a flock of scared birds flying every which way. I listen and listen.

"I don't believe I can spare him," Master Thomas says. "He's one of our best pickers and handy with machines. I'm thinking of teaching him how to keep the cotton gin in good repair."

I let out my breath and put my arms around Sue. Her daddy got sold away last year and she hasn't seen him since.

When I get home I hug my daddy hard and tell him the good news.

It's Saturday night. Mammy washes our clothes and near rubs the skin off us scrubbing us shiny clean for church.

We sit in the gallery. White folks sit below us in the church. When we sing "Amazing Grace" white folk and slaves sing together.

In the afternoon we go into the woods. Our church has a blue sky for the ceiling and green grass for the floor. We've got our own preacher. He tells the story of Moses who freed the people of Israel. "The good Lord's going to free us too," he promises. "The Jubilee is coming."

We sing "All God's Chillun Got Wings" and "Stand Still Jordan." We sing louder than the white folks to be sure the good Lord hears us. I hope He's listening.

We're listening when the boss tells Master Thomas a plow and some horses would get the work done faster than the hoe. That sounds good to us because the hoe is hard work.

The Master says he's not buying any plow. Slaves, he says, are cheaper than horses.

Tonight every candle in the great house is lit. It looks like they hung up the sun right inside the parlor. There's a party going on. Fiddles throw music out the windows.

Bobby, Sue, and me, Ella May, dance on the grass. We dance and dance until our feet are damp with dew and the whip-poor-will says it's time to go home.

Hallelujah! The last of the cotton is picked.

I get to help Daddy be a jumper today. They hang a big bag of cotton up and we climb right in. We jump and jump on the cotton. I dance the Turkey Trot and the Mary Jane. First the cotton is soft on my toes but when we're finished dancing that bale is hard packed.

That same night when we listen we hear Mistress Louise ask, "Why don't I start a little school for the slave children?"

Master Thomas says, "What can you be thinking, my dear? It's against the law to educate slaves."

The lady who teaches Mistress Grace has set her a poem to learn. She says it over and over for her mama.

> *And I will make thee beds of roses,*
> *And a thousand fragrant poesies,*
> *A cap of flowers, and a kirtle,*
> *Embroidered all with leaves of myrtle.*

I know roses and I know myrtle bushes, but I sure don't know what a kirtle is and neither do Bobby and Sue. I say the poem all the way home and now it's my poem, too.

When I go to sleep I pretend my scratchy straw mattress is a bed of roses.

Cold weather is coming so winter clothes get handed out. Bobby's got a shirt, Sue and me got a flannel dress and drawers. No new shoes. My toes won't like that.

Master Thomas is spied walking around in his uniform, brass buttons, sword and all.

Daddy tells me, “Ella May, you and Bobby and Sue need to listen extra hard tonight. I got a feeling dangerous times are coming. Could be our lives going to depend on what you children hear.”

Master Thomas is angry. His words come out mean as rattlesnakes. “I can’t believe Abraham Lincoln has been elected president,” Master says. “Lincoln is a madman! He says slavery is wrong! He says slavery must end!”

Bobby, Sue, and me, Ella May, run fast.

Our mammies and daddies gather around us. This time they do the listening. We tell them, “We got us a new president. Abraham Lincoln.”

Daddy says, “Moses is come! We’re going to be free like the children of Israel. It’s the Jubilee for sure!”

I ask Daddy, “Is our listening over?”

Daddy says, “We see the road, but we don’t see all the way to where the ending is. We got to know how long is that road and how we get down it. Bobby, Sue, and you, Ella May, your listening is just begun.”